Groundwood Books/Douglas & McIntyre
720 Bathurst Street, Suite 500
Toronto, Ontario M5S 2R4

Distributed in the USA by Publishers Group West
1700 Fourth Street
Berkeley, CA 94710

We acknowledge the financial support of the Canada Council for the Arts, the Ontario Arts Council and the Government of Canada through the Book Publishing Industry Development Program for our publishing activities.

Canadian Cataloguing in Publication Data
Gay, Marie-Louise
[Sur mon île. English]
On my island
A Groundwood book.
Translation of: Sur mon île.
ISBN 0-88899-396-X
I. Title. II. Title: Sur mon île. English.
PS8563.A868S9713 2000   jC843'.54   C00-930157-7
PZ7.G2375On 2000

Printed and bound in China by Everbest Printing Co. Ltd.

MARIE~LOUISE GAY

ON MY ISLAND

A GROUNDWOOD BOOK DOUGLAS & McINTYRE TORONTO VANCOUVER BUFFALO

I LIVE

ALONE
ON MY
ISLAND.

ALL ALONE,

WITH
A
WOLF,
TWO
CATS,
THREE
ANTS
AND
A . . . .

THERE'S NOT MUCH TO DO ON MY

ISLAND.

NOTHING HAPPENS. IT'S HOT. WE DRIFT AROUND AND AROUND AND AROUND...

WE OFTEN DREAM OF WILD

OF MYSTERIOUS HAPPENINGS AND ODD EVENTS.

BUT IT'S NO USE. ON MY ISLAND,

NOTHING EVER HAPPENS.

DAY AFTER DAY, THE WOLF GOES FISHING,

SO WE EAT A LOT OF FISH

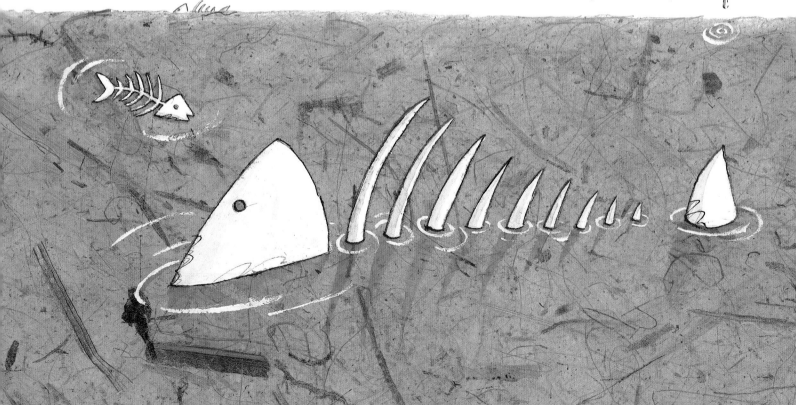

DAY IN AND DAY OUT

THE ANTS BUILD SANDCASTLES,

THEN THE RAIN

WASHES THEM AWAY.

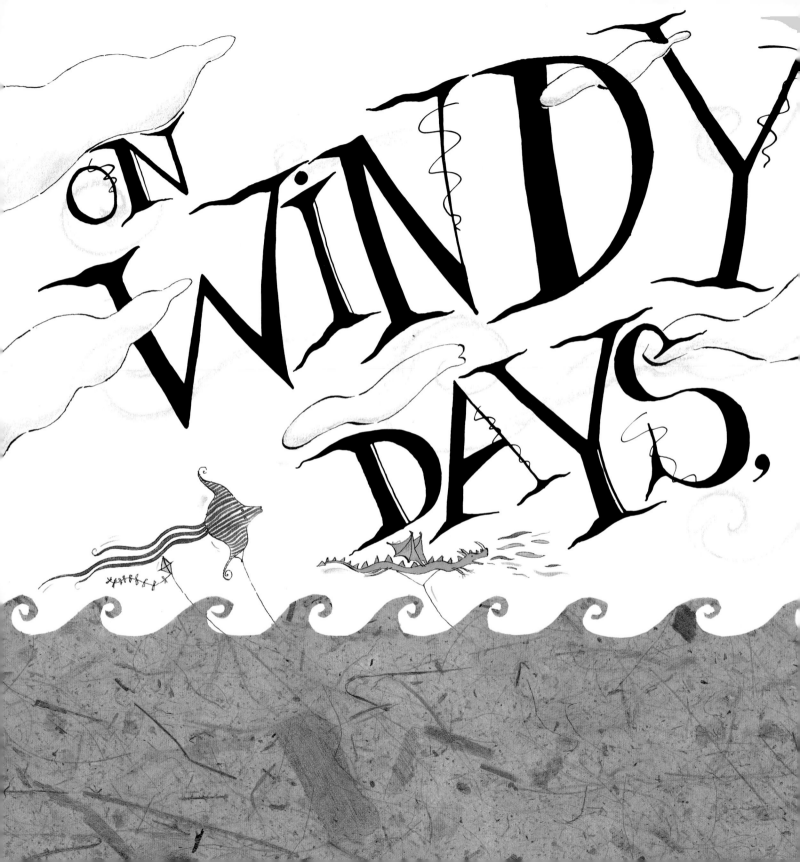

ON WINDY DAYS,

WINTER FOLLOWS

SUMMER,

AND NOTHING, ABSOLUTELY

NOTHING EVER HAPPENS,

ON MY ISLAND.

Position 1:

Position 2 and 3: